D0294228

Zoë and the Unicorn

For Pebbles, Herbie and Megan

First published in Great Britain in 2007
by Piccadilly Press Ltd.,
5 Castle Road, London NW1 8PR
www.piccadillypress.co.uk

Text designed by Louise Millar
Colour reproduction by Dot Gradations Ltd UK
Printed and bound in China by WKT.

ISBN: 978 1 85340 920 2 (hardback)
978 1 85340 915 8 (paperback)

1 3 5 7 9 10 8 6 4 2

A catalogue record of this book
is available from the British Library

Jane Andrews has two sons and lives in South Wales.
Piccadilly Press also publish the other books in this series:

ISBN: 1 85340 640 6 (p/b)

ISBN: 1 85340 651 1 (p/b)

ISBN: 1 85340 644 9 (p/b)

ISBN: 1 85340 726 7 (p/b)

ISBN: 1 85340 728 3 (p/b)

ISBN: 1 85340 744 5 (p/b)

ISBN: 1 85340 816 6 (p/b)

ISBN: 1 85340 838 7 (p/b)

Zoë and the Unicorn

Jane Andrews

Piccadilly Press • London

Early one morning, the Fairy Queen called Zoë and Pip to her bedside.
'I've been ill and now this entry form for the Annual Spells Competition is late,' said the Queen, in between coughs.
'You must get it to the Fairy Council by three o'clock today or we can't enter!'
'Don't worry, you can count on us,' Zoë said, taking the scroll.

Zoë and Pip waved goodbye to all the other fairies and flew off. The Fairy Council was on the other side of the forest, but they had plenty of time to get there.

'Isn't this wonderful?' said Pip, as they reached the forest. 'All the animals and the beautiful trees!'

Soon they were testing each other on the names of flowers and birds.

‘Look!’ said Zoë. ‘There’s a strange little bird. Isn’t it sweet?’

They began tiptoeing through the bushes to get a closer look. They followed the bird until it flew away, high into the trees.

‘Pip, is the path this way or that way?’ asked Zoë. Neither fairy knew which way to turn. The trees seemed to glare down at them.

‘We’re lost, Pip!’ said Zoë, trembling.

The forest seemed dark and scary as
Zoë and Pip searched in vain for the path.
Suddenly Zoë gasped in horror. 'Oh Pip, I've lost my bag
with the scroll!'

They looked everywhere.

Under bushes, in the trees, behind the toadstools.
But they couldn't find the bag anywhere.

Zoë and Pip didn't know what to do. They sank to the ground in a tired heap and cried.

Then, through their tears, they saw a strange mist moving towards them...

There was the most beautiful unicorn!
Zoë and Pip were amazed.

Somehow Zoë and Pip knew the unicorn had come to help them. Without saying a word, the unicorn knelt down so they could climb up on his back.

It wasn't long before they found Zoë's bag hanging on a tree branch.

'We must hurry or we'll be late!' said Zoë, holding tightly on to her bag.
The unicorn stretched out his wings and off they flew, high over the forest and all the way to the Fairy Council.

While the unicorn waited nearby,
Zoë and Pip ran into the Fairy Council.
The Fairy Councillor took the scroll.
Just then, the clock struck three.

‘You fairies are lucky,’ said the Fairy Councillor sternly.
‘One more moment and you would have been too late!’

The sun was setting as the unicorn brought Zoë and Pip down on the edge of the forest near Fairy School.

Both the fairies hugged the unicorn.
'Can't you stay with us?' asked Zoë.
The unicorn didn't answer, but just shook his head.
'Maybe his luck will stay with us,' whispered Pip as they waved goodbye.

The Fairy Queen thanked
Zoë and Pip.
'I hope you had a good
journey,' she said.

'Oh yes!' said Zoë and Pip together.